For Bob and Jane, who never met a question unworthy of an answer — D.B.

For my motormouth-Max brothers. Thanks for not casting any spells on me! — D.H.

TEXT COPYRIGHT © 2014 BY DAN BAR-EL
LLLUSTRATIONS COPYRIGHT © 2014 BY DAVID HUYCK

Published in Canada by Tundra Books, a division of Random House of Canada Limited,
One Toronto Street, Suite 300, Toronto, Ontario M5C 2V6

Published in the United States by Tundra Books of Northern New York,
P.O. Box 1030, Plattsburgh, New York 12901

Library of Congress Control Number: 2013940753

LIBRARY AND ARCHIVES CANADA CATALOGUING IN PUBLICATION

Bar-el, Dan, author
Nine words Max / by Dan Bar-el ; illustrated by David Huyck.

Issued in print and electronic formats.
ISBN 978-1-77049-562-3 (bound).—ISBN 978-1-77049-564-7 (epub)

I. Huyck, David, 1976-, illustrator II. Title.

PS8553.A76229N56 2014   jC813'.54   C2013-903527-3   C2013-903528-1

Edited by Samantha Swenson
Designed by David Huyck and Tundra Books
The artwork in this book was rendered digitally with sensors and doohickeys and magic.
The text was set in Scala Sans, Hank BT and Blockhead Unplugged.

www.tundrabooks.com

Printed and bound in China

1 2 3 4 5 6   19 18 17 16 15 14

NINE WORDS MAX

Written by **Dan Bar-el**   Illustrated by **David Huyck**

Tundra Books

Maximilian was a prince who asked questions ...

Why is the sky blue? How do bears decide when to hibernate? Can we ever really know the future? What is the warmest spot in the world? Do lentils give you nightmares? Who invented socks? Do hermits talk to themselves? If a tree fell on a florist ...

Maximilian was also a prince who knew answers ...

Lutes were once played in Egypt. The square root of nine is three. Diamonds are the hardest substance on earth. The Atlantic Ocean is more salty than the Pacific Ocean. Minerva is the goddess of wisdom. Equinox means equal night. Squirrels are never to be trusted.

And between all
these questions and
answers, Maximilian
was a prince who
took great pleasure
in sharing what
was on his mind.

It's been said that a butterfly's flapping wings
might cause a storm on the other side of the
world. Eggs cannot be unscrambled, and you
should never put them all in one basket.
Everywhere around us are sounds, but at
some point there was suddenly music too.
If all the world's a stage, then we should be
wearing more makeup.

Maximilian had three older brothers, Kurt, Wilt and Tripp. They were princes too, but more simple in design. They were not big on questions. They had no interest in answers. Conversation was something they preferred to avoid altogether.

I've noticed, brothers, that you do an awful lot of yawning. "Yawn" comes from the Old English word *yanen* or *yonen*. Some say that yawns are infectious. If one person yawns, then it is likely that their companion will yawn too. But is it really contagious like a cold or flu? I was speaking with Matilda, the wool merchant, who believes that yawning is caused by sheep —

Maximilian, would you

please stop

talking.

The three princes liked to spend their mornings hanging around the covered market looking as bored as bored princes could look. Maximilian tried to act bored, but life was just too interesting.

In the afternoons, Kurt, Wilt and Tripp would send pointless messages back and forth to other princes. Maximilian tried to keep his short and silly, but there was just so much to say.

babbling!

Maximilian, would you

just *stop*

NUH-UH

NO U R!

BRB LOL

UR SO

TAKE IT BACK!

Dear Prince Dusty, I hope you are having an
enjoyable day as the weather is quite pleasant.
But I noticed that the sky in the east was red this morning,
which can only mean that rain is on the way. I like the color red.
In China, red is the color of courage. In other lands, red is the
color of love. I wonder if somewhere in the world red
is the color for laziness or indigestion or —

Why is that puppet hitting the other puppet with lumber? That wood doesn't look very strong. Maybe it's northern white cedar, which is a softwood. Snakewood is one of the hardest woods in the world. I hear it grows in Australia. If we lived in Australia, it would be a completely different season right now because it lies below the equator. Do you think they have puppet shows down there? I bet the puppets have terrible headaches on account of getting hit with snakewood —

zip your

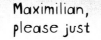

Maximilian, please just

lips!

In the evenings, the three older princes would sprawl on the royal couch and watch hours upon hours of puppet shows. Despite his best efforts to fit in, Maximilian could not sit and stare silently at the box.

One day, the king and queen made an announcement.
"We're going on holiday. Be good princes and look
after the kingdom, would you?"

Too much talking!

All day!

Boring!

The three older brothers
saw an opportunity.
Here was their chance
to finally put a stop to
Maximilian's constant
chattering. They rushed
over to the royal wizard
and demanded action.

"I could cast a spell to make him speak only ten words at a time," the wizard suggested.

Even ten would be too much.

So the wizard turned his spell up a notch.

That evening at dinner, the three princes tested it out.

Maximilian was thrilled at the sudden interest in his life. He stood up to speak.

And then he sat down and went back to eating his mashed potatoes.
He noticed his brothers were still staring.

The spell worked! Maximilian could speak only nine words at a time.
The three princes snickered in delight. They were finally free of long-winded speeches.
Now they could stand around, sit around or lie around and not be forced to think
about one tiny thing. For Kurt, Wilt and Tripp, life was perfect …

. . . Until word arrived of a visit by Queen Spark of the land of Flint, the first visit in many, many generations.

Flintians were very particular and easily offended. Peace depended upon a smooth show of respect. Failure to do so meant certain war. Of course, the older princes had never paid attention to the minor details. Only Maximilian had ever shown interest in learning the Flintian ways, which he made sure to share with the kingdom.

When the queen arrives, flags must point toward the . . .

To the royal artillery, he ordered,

Then he walked away.

But were flags to point north, south, east or west? Were cannons to blast every two steps or every two hours? This was not good.

Maximilian visited the castle kitchen.

To the royal cook, he ordered,

Then he left the kitchen.

But did Flintian bread need sesame seeds or cinnamon? Were they not to serve fish or figs? This was not good at all.

And finally, to the whole court, he said,

Maximilian now felt satisfied that all had been explained.

But were sad songs to be avoided or sappy songs? Were balls not to be juggled or bricks? And what exactly *were* they to wiggle?

Oh, this was really not good.

A scout galloped toward the castle. "The warrior queen arrives!
She comes with her army!"

Maximilian and his brothers watched the massive Flintian army emerge
over the far hills. From the center came Queen Spark, followed closely
by her solemn attendants.

Maximilian nodded to the troops to lift their flags.

He winked at the royal artillery to shoot their cannons.

But no one moved. No one breathed. So terrified were they of making a mistake, they all stood frozen in fear.

Inside the banquet hall, the queen was seated at the table of honor. Maximilian summoned the baker to bring the bread. He beckoned to the cook to serve the meal.

But again no one moved. The fear of causing a war turned them into statues.

Hoping to offer some pleasant distraction, Maximilian called over the singers to sing and the jugglers to juggle. Yet no note was sung and no object juggled. The entertainers were also afraid of offending the queen.

But offended she was.

"You call this hospitality?"
Queen Spark yelled. "Is there
not one gesture of friendship
you can offer me?"

The three older princes were stumped and worried.
They looked to Maximilian for an answer.

Reluctantly, Kurt, Wilt and Tripp stood up and walked before the queen. They gazed imploringly at the members of the court, looking for some hint of what they should do. Everyone shrugged their shoulders.

"Well?" demanded Queen Spark.

Kurt wiggled his ears.   Wilt wiggled his nose.   Tripp wiggled his bum.

Queen Spark exploded in rage. She turned upon the princes. "How dare you! How DARE you! I am your guest and yet you mock my customs by wiggling everything *but* your fingers! Prepare yourself for battle!" And she marched toward the door.

Queen Spark looked down and found the three princes wrapped around her legs. "Well? What have you to say?"

Like three leaky faucets, Kurt, Wilt and Tripp gushed out an explanation, using more words than they had ever used in their entire lives.

Queen Spark could take it no longer. "My, how your brothers blather on, Prince Maximilian! But they say nothing and only waste my time."

By now, the royal wizard had told Maximilian about the spell.

His three brothers begged the wizard to reverse it.

Maximilian turned to the Flintian queen, bowed deeply and uttered exactly nine words.

The three princes held their breath, praying desperately that Maximilian would speak some more.

And speak he did. He started by instructing everyone on how to host Flintian royalty in the proper manner.

Then, offering the queen his arm, Prince Maximilian led her around the castle grounds and spoke long and elegantly.

'There is nothing on this earth more to be prized than true friendship,' suggested dear Saint Thomas. And didn't Aristotle say that wishing to be friends is quick work, but friendship itself is like a slow, ripening fruit? Our two kingdoms have been friends a very long time, Queen Spark.

The young prince spoke for a whole hour and a half. His brothers listened respectfully. The queen's smile grew brighter and brighter.

Afterward, a meal was served complete with Flintian grasshopper bread and macaroni and cheese without cheese. They were entertained by a collection of extremely sad songs followed by the juggling of everything but cats.

Finally, as the cannons rang out every two minutes and the flags were pointed west toward the red setting sun, the whole court bid Queen Spark farewell. Led by Kurt, Wilt and Tripp, everyone wiggled their fingers fondly.